For more information about this book and other anthologies,
please visit bit.ly/didcotwriters

Compositions

a collection of short stories on the theme of music

edited by Alice Little

Contents

Mariella and the Singing Flute

by Margaret Gallop

Mariella lived with her brothers in a cottage in the dark wood. One day the oldest brother said, 'I must go and find work,' and he said a tearful goodbye. 'You are safe here little sister. Neighbours pass by every day.'

A year later her second brother left to go and make his fortune. 'Beware of strangers, little Mariella.'

Another year later a tall man walked by and sat on the stone outside her cottage. She watched him. After a while he picked up his sack and walked on down the forest path. Mariella stepped hesitantly out and looked after him. He had left something on the stone, it was a little flute. Should she call out, or pick it up and follow him? She did neither, but after a while she put it to her lips and blew. It played a tune she had never heard before and it seemed to be talking to her.

Far away your true love lies.
Leave your warm fire, go find your future.

Mariella wondered if she should she listen to the flute and follow the stranger down the road. She tried playing it again.

Beware, beware of leaving your home.
Stay in your small safe place, Mariella.

What should she do?

One day a beautiful doe walked past her door. Mariella felt restless and picked up the flute.

Follow the doe though the wakening wood.
Follow her gold tail flickering through shadows.

Mariella hesitated and played again.

Beware, beware of greedy eyes.
Beware of the knife in the dark.

Mariella peeped out of the window. The doe seemed to be waiting for her. She hung the flute round her neck and followed the doe along the forest path. They walked through dark woods and open glades, over meadow pasture and rippling brooks. She slept against the doe's flank and climbed on her back when they crossed streams. One day they came to a watermill. Mariella asked the miller's wife if there was somewhere to sleep.

The miller's wife welcomed them. 'What a gift you have brought me. We'll have a feast tomorrow.'

'Oh no,' said Mariella, 'the doe is my friend. But where can we shelter tonight?'

The miller's wife put them in an outhouse which leant against the mill. That night Mariella woke to see the old woman creep in from the mill with a gleaming knife. Mariella pushed the heavy outer door open and the doe slipped out into the darkness.

'So,' said the woman, 'you've cheated me. You must work for me and sleep under the table.'

One morning she sent Mariella to pluck watercress from the river bank. A large fish swam up to Mariella, she took out her flute and played.

Go, go with the glimmering fish,
his shimmering scales, his shining eyes.

She hesitated and played again.

Don't risk the river, the rocky falls.
Beware of its swirls and the fisherman's hook.

Mariella pondered a moment. Then she left the watermill and followed the giant fish up the river. She swam in the river, scrambled up rocks and rode on the great fish as he leapt the waterfalls. They came to a bridge where a fisherman stood with his line.

'Here, little girl, you have brought me a wonderful fish.'

'No,' said Mariella, 'do not hurt him.'

The man laughed. 'Get out of my way so I can cast my line.'

Mariella jumped off the fish's back and swam towards the fisherman, fighting the river current. The great fish leapt through the water and disappeared under the bridge.

The fisherman man shook his fist at Mariella. She ran up the path until he was out of sight. As she walked along the river bank she noticed a boy with golden hair ahead of her. She took out her flute.

Go, go with the golden-haired boy,
a friend for life and a prince in hiding.

Then she played again for the warning.

Danger awaits the golden-haired boy.
Envy and murder are waiting for him.

Mariella thought about the doe and the fish. She caught up with him.

'Who are you?' he asked.

'I am Mariella and I have nothing but a flute.'

The boy blinked, 'I too have nothing, but I believe I am the true son of a king.'

Then they both laughed.

'I will come with you to claim your kingdom.'

'I fear it will not be safe. Another man claims my place.'

'I will come.'

As they entered the town an open coach followed them through the stone gate. A man in red velvet stood up in the coach. 'Bow, bow you people!' he shouted. 'Your king requires your obeisance.'

'No I don't,' mumbled the old king beside him, 'but there's no stopping this young upstart. Would that my first wife's child had survived. He might have taken better care of my people.'

The golden-haired boy didn't bow.

'You, peasant!' shouted the prince. 'Who are you to disregard me?'

'I have come to claim my rightful place in this kingdom.'

'Seize him!' yelled the prince. 'Bring him to the castle.'

'Now, that young man looks more like it,' muttered the old king to himself. 'Stands up for himself. Reminds me of my first wife.' He wept a little.

The castle gate closed to Mariella, so she followed the river path under the castle walls.

Inside, the prince took the boy to the river terrace where the king liked to sit.

'So?' said the prince.

'I have come to claim my lawful inheritance.'

'Your lawful inheritance?'

He turned to the king. 'I am the son of your first queen, Wilhelmina, your majesty.'

The prince roared and slapped the boy's face.

'Your evidence?' asked the king.

'This ring, tied round my neck, which belonged to my mother.'

The prince grabbed the ring and twisted the cord lifting the boy off the ground.

'Couldn't he just take it off?' asked the king wearily.

The boy knelt and gave it to the king.

'That looks very like….'

'Fraud,' yelled the prince. He grabbed the ring and threw it over the wall and it splashed into the river.

'Destroying evidence?' muttered the king.

'The boy is a trickster,' said the prince. 'Put him in the tower.'

Mariella was playing her flute by the river bank. The water stirred and a large fish tossed the ring on its cord back up to her. 'Thank you, fish,' she cried.

After dark she climbed lightly up to the boy's stone window. As she looked in, a figure with a long knife stood over the boy's bed. The moon flashed against the flute and blinded the wicked prince for a moment so that his knife stabbed into the bedframe. He yelled with frustration, the guards ran in.

'Guards, catch this intruder!'

Next day the prince summoned the king to witness the execution of the boy.

'Must we?' asked the king.

'Your majesty, last night an intruder attempted to free him.'

'Let me see this intruder.'

The guards brought in Mariella.

'Please let her go,' said the boy, 'she was trying to help me.'

'By stabbing you?'

'No, she didn't have the knife, she had a flute.'

'How charming. Let me hear her play.'

As Mariella started to play, a doe and a stag leapt onto the terrace.

Mariella put her arms round the doe's neck.

'Grab those deer!' yelled the prince.

'No,' cried Mariella.

The stag dipped its horns and tossed the prince over the wall and into the river.

'Oh, well done,' murmured the king. 'This is more like it.'

'If only you had the ring,' he said out loud.

Mariella took the ring from her neck and, kneeling, offered it to the king.

The king stood up. 'Guards, release my long-lost son. My second wife told me you died at birth, along with my wife. She brought her own son instead.

'Now, what shall we do with him? What he planned for you?'

'Please be merciful.'

'That's just what Wilhelmina would have said. I now have three proofs you are my true son.'

The prince dragged himself, wet and furious, back into the courtyard.

'So, how shall we punish the prince? Perhaps your friend

could pay her flute while we think?'

Mariella lifted the flute to her lips. The words were clear to everyone this time.

Go, prince, go to your mother's land,
High king of all you could be.

The prince started, then stared at the flute. Then shouted for his best horse.

'Wait…' said Mariella, but the prince strode away, mounted his horse and galloped out of the castle, grabbing the flute as he passed Mariella.

'Oh, it wasn't mine to give!'

In response, a tall courtier stepped forward. 'Mariella, the flute was yours. Your brothers asked me to give it to you when I passed your cottage, but you were too shy to come out.'

'My brothers?'

'Yes, they are in this town.'

Mariella smiled with pleasure.

'You will be reunited with your brothers,' smiled the king, 'but what can I grant *you*, my neglected son?'

'May I choose a bride, your majesty?'

'Of course.'

'Mariella?'

'Oh,' said Mariella. 'I don't have the flute to ask.'

The king and his son laughed. 'Take your time, Mariella.'

Mariella took her time to make up her mind, and she never regretted the decision she made.

The End

The Song that Solved the Case

by Zoe Reed

Inspector Murray was sitting at his desk going through his notes on the Ashby case, the girl had been missing for eight months now and he was losing hope that she would ever be found.

He needed a distraction, and as chance would have it at that moment Constable Hughes knocked on his door.

'Sorry to bother you, Inspector, but we've had a report of gunfire in a house on Oaktree Lane. We've cordoned off the area but I'm afraid it's a bit of a mess, sir. Two dead bodies. We thought it might be best if you took a look'.

Inspector Murray followed him to the car, which they had started using since the village had begun expanding, just after the war. It seemed people were much keener on living in the countryside these days.

The drive was short but by the time they were halfway there Hughes had filled him in on most of the details. A young woman and a man had been found. The man had an ex-army pistol on him and it appeared he had shot the woman and then himself. The motive, however, was unclear and that was why the Inspector had been called: he was known for finding the smallest of clues and building up the picture around a case, although the Ashby case had thrown him somewhat and he had started to think his mind was not as sharp as it used to be.

It had been late-summer last year when Elizabeth Ashby's mother, Margaret, rushed frantically into the station. She was hysterical, and it took them an hour to calm her down. Inspector Muray had spoken to her when she was ready, and he could still remember the desperate look in her eyes as she told him of her daughter, aged seven, who had disappeared. Elizabeth had been playing in the garden and when her mother looked up from washing the dishes, she was gone.

Their house backed onto some woods, and of course they had searched them thoroughly, but found nothing. Neighbours had been questioned, houses visited and yet no one had seen or heard anything. It seemed she had vanished into thin air, and it bothered the Inspector that there was no obvious line of enquiry to follow, no clue as to what happened that day.

'Inspector, we're here. If you're ready?'

The Inspector nodded and climbed out of the car.

The house was a picturesque place, the building itself was nothing special, but the attention to detail in the front garden was astonishing. Ivy crept up the house, hugging the front windows and arching over the door as if by design. A small, well-kept flower bed either side of the path leading up to the house was filled with an assortment of beautiful plants, some in full bloom, others flowerless, but creating a backdrop for those that were blossoming in the mild spring weather. It certainly wasn't what you would think of as the scene of a murder.

The Inspector sighed to himself, made his way up to the door and entered the house. The first thing he noticed once inside was the music coming from the living room.

'I assume that was playing when you arrived?' he asked.

'Yes, sir, we thought it best to leave everything as it was. I can turn it off if you like? Sorry, it did seem a bit inappropriate. It's been playing on repeat since we got here.'

'No, it may be useful,' the Inspector replied.

It certainly was inappropriate, he knew the song, everyone did, a favourite from Bing Crosby: 'You are my Sunshine'.

Murray took in the two bodies. The young woman lay on her back, eyes staring up at the ceiling. She was beautiful, blonde waves framed her face and she wore a pretty, white floral dress. Such a waste of a life, the Inspector thought. No matter how many times he had seen this sort of thing, it still saddened him.

Now, the man on the other hand was almost the opposite: scruffily dressed, an unkempt beard that looked as though it was long overdue a trim. The rest of his face was a little harder to make out due to the gunshot wound. There was nothing in his pockets, just the pistol in his hand. The Inspector began his search of the house.

It soon became clear that the woman lived there alone, but judging by the pictures all around her house she had a loving family. They would need to be informed, Murray thought.

It turned out she was a nurse at the village hospital – if you could call it that. They had all the basic facilities, but for anything major it was a two-hour drive to the main hospital.

Murray was beginning to think he would find no clue here as to who this man was, when he came upon a stack of letters on the dresser. He started to read them, and the thought occurred to him that this man might be the writer of these letters. The first one was written about a month ago, enquiring as to how she was, thanking her for all her help and asking if perhaps she would like to go out for dinner. He was in the next village over and would be happy to visit.

The Inspector guessed that she had not replied as the next letter, dated a week later, was harsher in tone, demanding that she answer him, after all the time they had spent together.

And then it became clear, when he used the term 'rehabilitation', that he had been a patient of hers. Seemed he had a leg wound from the war and she had been helping him with some physiotherapy.

A few more letters followed, becoming increasingly aggressive, until the last, dated a few days ago. It was really quite hostile, and ended with, 'If I can't have you then no one can, for it seems you will never know how much I love you'. As Murray read those words he heard them sound downstairs from the record player and suddenly it all made sense.

The Inspector returned to the other officers and addressed them.

'It seems that what we have here is an act of unrequited love. If I'm right, this man was James Stone, he lived in the village down the road and was a patient of the woman, Nancy Brown, who was a nurse at the hospital. He left perhaps a month ago, and somehow found out her address: possibly he followed her home one evening, we may never know.

'He proceeded to write a series of letters to Nancy which we can, for now, assume she ignored. Thus, he became gradually angrier and more unpleasant in his writing. The last letter he wrote contained what seems to be a threat, along with a reference to the song that is now playing.

'I think we can deduce from this that he came here uninvited and maybe convinced Nancy to let him in or used force to enter her home, where he confronted her. She, I imagine, stood her ground and refused to accept this man's feelings for her, and so, in his rage, he shot her, as he desired that if he could not be with her then no one could have her.

'After this, he put on the record, setting it to repeat, to symbolise his whole take on the situation, loving her, or more rightly obsessing over her, but not having her in reality. I believe he then took his own life because he could not live without her. I think that's everything.'

The other officers looked astonished at how quickly Murray had pieced this all together.

'Well done, Inspector, that was some intelligent thinking. I think we can take it from here if that's OK?' Hughes said.

The Inspector agreed to this and moved towards the door, then hesitated for a second. Something in that song was bothering him. It was a happy song, to him it reminded him of summer, sunshine, being outdoors, playing outdoors as a child in fact.

That's when it hit him: playing outside, that's what Margaret Ashby said her daughter had been doing on that fateful day. Why hadn't he realised before? It was so obvious: she couldn't have been playing outside that day, it had been, for a summer's day, utterly miserable, raining all morning. It had been a break in what had otherwise been a remarkably nice summer.

That meant the mother had been lying, and why would she lie if not to cover up the truth? – a truth the Inspector suspected would not bring a happy resolution to the case.

He would go straight to the mother's house to bring her in.

He had the music to thank: the song that had solved not one but two cases that day.

An Unforgivable Act of Generosity

by Jan Brown

Never date a collector. I speak from bitter experience. Unless you're on the same track as train-spotters, collectors are beyond normal human comprehension. I had the misfortune to date a record collector in my innocence. I say misfortune now; at the time I was naive, blinkered by love and lust. I listened to bands I'd never heard of, admired freaky artwork and faked interest in sleeve notes. That's what good girlfriends do.

I've been thinking about the warning signs I missed.

One: likely to be a total control freak regarding anything vinyl-related. I knew exactly which albums I was allowed to play and which were off limits. I was taught how to handle vinyl using only the pad of my thumb and middle finger, for fear of the dreaded finger mark. I learnt that the inner sleeve wasn't just a bit of paper with a pointless hole in; it was an intrinsic part of the whole album and must never be forced into a space it might be reluctant to fill – and, believe me, inner sleeves often put up a fight. When I chose an album to play, I marked the location with a slip of paper to ensure it would always be returned to where it belonged, according to a system unique and comprehensible only to my boyfriend.

Two: there may be obsessive-compulsive symptoms. Albums alphabetised on custom-made shelves in a temperature-regulated room, many not there to be touched, let alone played. Just there. Immaculate, hand-written catalogues with every minute detail transcribed, pored over daily and updated with each acquisition. Once a book was filled, a new one would be purchased but it had to be identical: black cloth, hard cover, A4, a hundred pages. An inordinate amount of time spent on esoteric websites, tracking down deluxe editions, elusive new pressings, illicit recordings, maybe the rare album with the misprint that got withdrawn. Did you know there's an early Beatles worth a small fortune because they printed Lennon and McArtney? Do you care? Apparently one should – such things are valuable.

Three: probably no idea about desirable presents but unfailingly generous with home-made CDs of rare downloaded tracks no one else would want to hear. Not me anyway. In my case, these CDs had to be played, usually in the car to and from work, because a quiz invariably followed (see Four). They were sweetly left on the pillow while I slept, a loving offering comparable to the mangled vole your cat might drop at your feet. The same flummoxed eyes when I expressed my thanks in underwhelmed tones which silently said, 'I'd rather have roses'. At least I didn't scream like I did at the vole.

Four: not the best conversationalist; in fact, a probable absence of people-skills. My boyfriend would often embark on one-sided discourse (for discourse, read lecture) over 'romantic' dinners, about what missing tracks had to be located, what constituted a reasonable price, what he could get if he didn't have to pay for half this meal. What did I think of the CD he made me? He wasn't trying to catch me out, he genuinely cared.

Oh, Four-B: a distinct need always to be right. To be fair, he generally was, but a total intolerance of anyone who claimed to have 'all the U2 stuff' when he could be pretty certain they were completely unaware of the extensive catalogue of U2 stuff that didn't reach the charts. Charts were anathema.

Five: cautious with money. Not a bad thing but, OK, tight-fisted. Never given to spontaneous expenditure because there was a strict budget and most of it was allocated to The Collection. Which brings me to...

Six: zero interest in fashion and incapable of brushing up well for more formal occasions; at least, not without assistance. A wardrobe of jeans, T-shirts (usually from gigs), button-down shirts in a vast range of shades of blue and grey, and Doc Martens. Smart meant putting on a suit jacket from the charity shop and swapping blue for black denim. Maybe a buff of the ancient bovver boots with his sleeve.

Seven: complete and utter heartlessness. He dumped me over a record. If I'd scratched a Comsat Angels or made dinky flowerpot holders out of melted Grateful Deads, I'd have understood. To explain, I was visiting my mum and asked if I could rummage among Dad's old stuff in the attic. I found something I thought my collector boyfriend might appreciate. I was so chuffed. I was no longer an outsider – I'd located a gem.

I rang him straight away.

'Guess what I've found.'

'Oh God, not a lump?'

(That's Eight, by the way: a tendency always to think the

worst.)

'No, silly. Listen. Remember I said Dad was into Dylan in his youth? He used to talk about how he visited New York – bragged about buying some Dylan album that got withdrawn?'

'The Freewheelin' Bob Dylan,' he replied like a computer. '1963, Colombia. Four tracks left off later pressings. Replaced with others but no one knows why. Stamped with 1A. Worth a fortune, but you can't find it for love nor money.'

(Nine: full of information of negligible interest to others, generously shared; oblivious to numbed reactions.)

'Maybe not for money, sweetheart, definitely for love. I've got it here in my hand.'

There was stunned silence, a strangled moan, more silence. I could picture him struggling with his astonishment, the mental gymnastics as he cross-checked his catalogues with the online information he visualised, and I positively glowed. Surely, this was worth an engagement ring!

'Yep, Dad had a copy and it's yours, sweetheart.'

'Stereo or mono?' I should have expected that. I knew where to look by now. He'd trained me well.

'Stereo.'

'I don't know what to say.' That was good enough for me. He was happy.

'And Mum's written a little inscription on the cover for you: Dad's name and then "given to Adam, with our love". Isn't that sweet?'

More stunned silence.

'Well, aren't you excited?' I felt a bit miffed.

'Have you any idea what that means?' I flinched at the cold anger. 'That was worth twenty or thirty thousand pounds. It's worthless now.' He slammed down the phone.

He dumped me by text. Next day, all my belongings were delivered by a very embarrassed friend of ours who didn't know where to look or what to say. Actually, I say all my belongings: my albums weren't there. They'd been appropriated, absorbed into his collection. Eventually I would Google 'Freewheelin'' and realise the enormity of the desecration. But it wasn't about the money for him; it was the ownership. With a few strokes of Mum's pen, his dreams were shattered like an old 78 dropped on a scullery floor. But it confirmed for me that one should never date a collector.

Ten: unforgiving.

Theme and Variations

by Alice Little

I was born, if we can call it that, in Paris, circa 1889. I can't be precise because in the workshop individual pieces might be left for some time before being assembled into a violin.

My first owner was a music student at the Conservatoire. He came from a prominent Russian family, and he took me back east when he finished his studies. Sometimes we played classical music, but I preferred the nights spent playing Klezmer for his friends to dance to, stamping their feet and clapping their hands, swirling scarves and laughing together. I took several knocks at crowded gatherings, but I was young and it didn't seem to matter.

At the turn of the century, when he had children of his own I was passed to his son. The boy had soft fingers, but eventually we mastered his exercises. When the son grew up he took me west once more, to Berlin: a city broken after the Great War, where the winters were nearly as cold as in Russia. There he became a mathematics professor, performing at weekends for his friends, but we didn't play the old tunes any more.

The professor's own son was only twelve when I was passed down to the next generation, on the eve of a new war.

The boy had barely started learning to play, but his shoulders were strong and he had confidence. I had never been held like that before.

We left Berlin suddenly, crushed among children on a noisy train. Having crossed the North Sea we were stopped by an official who thought the boy planned to sell me for cash upon arrival in England. I was stunned by the very idea: was I not his own violin, a tangible connection to his Russian grandfather, something familiar to hold in his new life far from home?

'His parents gave him the violin because he likes to play,' our escort said, standing at the head of a queue of children, in front of the British customs officers.

'Play then,' a guard said brusquely.

The boy lifted me to his shoulder and bowed the strings. I sang as sweetly as I could, trying to help prove he could play. Then, recognising the tune, I switched to a bold, strong tone. The guards stood to attention. The tune was 'God Save the King'. We played three verses. They let us pass.

We saw out the war as peacefully as we could, and I went with the boy afterwards when he found work on a farm in Cambridgeshire. We didn't play much: I suppose he only kept me because I'd been given to him by his father. I lay dejectedly in my wooden case for many years, wrapped in my old silk scarf. I didn't like the dampness of the seasons in England but over the years I adjusted and no harm was done. The boy – no longer a boy – lived another forty years, and when he died I was sold to an antiques shop, my strings rusted and broken but otherwise I was still in good condition.

I next belonged to a young French academic who liked the thought of playing the violin more than the realities of practice. She collected beautiful things and spotted me as soon as I went on display in the shop. She saw that my maker's label was Parisian, like herself, and did not guess that in fact I spoke many languages.

I spent the university terms lounging on top of her piano: her friends would play sonatas with me when they came over for tea. She knew about instruments and kept me in good condition for her friends, but it wasn't the same as being with one person, developing a rapport. I longingly recalled the intense Russian tunes, the soft fingers of the professor, and even that brave anthem of the boy, short-lived though the moment had been.

The young French academic gained her doctorate, and stayed in Cambridge to work in a museum. She died suddenly in middle age, and her relatives donated all her instruments to the museum's collection.

My bow was taken away for a special exhibition, and I was shut in my old-fashioned case on a high shelf in the storeroom: not rare enough to be of interest to researchers, but old enough to be worth preserving. I was occasionally lent to students when their own instruments were out for repairs, but it was a quiet life.

Then just last week I found myself on the move again, this time heading to Turkey, where I had been promised to a teenager. The boy had left his home in a hurry and, arriving in a new town with no school to attend, no books to read, and nothing better to do, he had taken up playing the violin: teaching himself from online videos, using a beaten-up instrument he had found by chance.

The museum in Cambridge, hearing his story, had sought out a decent instrument to send to him: one that wasn't too valuable, but good enough for a serious student of music. Little did they know that this was the sort of work I had become accustomed to, the sort of journey I had been making all my life.

First I was spruced up, a bow was found, and I was placed in a special protective case. Then – a strange sensation – we flew south, to a place I had never been before, where the air is dry and the music is wild.

The boy's hands are rough, but he has strong fingers and knows how to make a melody dance. He has written a number of tunes especially for me, and we join in with songs on the radio: he can't sing along, he doesn't understand the words.

So here I am, over a century old, still travelling the world and learning new music. And though our current home is only temporary, I have found my own new home with him.

Facing the Music

by Alice Lam

The woman stepped back from the chipped and smudged mirror in the service station toilets. Her mismatched ensemble – navy blue trousers, black jacket and plain white blouse – felt like an extension of her discombobulated self. She blotted at the sheen of sweat on her face and neck, and hurried back to the bus.

Brown and wrinkled as well-worn leather, the driver made a show of looking at his watch, and opened the door for her. She had barely sat down before the bus pulled away. She was the only passenger. He did not think her worth the trouble.

After several hours, during which the woman napped fitfully, she was dropped off at the gate. The afternoon sun blasted her face as she walked up the drive and into the building.

The security guard was stout, balding. 'Photo ID,' he barked. She passed him her driving licence. He looked through her as he passed it back, then pointed to a small camera. 'Iris scan,' he said, slightly more gently.

The next guard gestured her through a metal detector, her belongings were X-rayed, then she was made to walk down a corridor where air puffed at her body for concealed drugs.

The doors slammed shut behind her, making her jump. Finally, she was patted down and allowed into the Visitor Reception Centre.

'Sorry, no food allowed,' said the receptionist.

'But it's sealed in plastic, it's a gift,' said the woman. 'I've carried it all day, I can show you the receipt.'

'Doesn't anyone read the website? No food without prior approval.' He passed her a key. 'Put your stuff in a locker. You'll be called soon.'

Summarily dismissed, the woman scanned the rows of moulded plastic chairs, and found one that faced away from the television.

'Meredith Black,' called the receptionist after half an hour. 'You can go through the door now.'

*

She walked into a controlled hubbub, a young mother trying to soothe a crying baby, two toddlers and an older woman, a priest, an elderly couple. The walls were painted in an uninspiring shade of beige, a handful of children's drawings providing welcome splashes of colour. It reminded her of an eighties school classroom. She sat at the remaining free table and waited.

She knew it was him even though it had been years. He shuffled towards her, lean and lanky, and sat opposite her. His back was hunched, head bowed, palms down on the table.

'Joe,' she said, gently placing her hand over his cold one.

He did not look up. She could see his breathing was quick, shallow.

'It's okay, I don't know what to do either. Here's the deal. We'll muddle along together, all right?'

He slipped his hand away, stole a furtive look around him, then returned to his slumped posture. He looked even younger than his thirty years.

'How're you doing?' Silence. 'You hungry?'

'Mm-hmm.'

'You want something from the vending machine? I brought you a cake but the bastards took it away for themselves.' She whispered the last part, and her heart leapt when he grinned shyly back at her. 'Chocolate, or a drink?'

He seemed to be more relaxed when she returned to the table with a small mound of snacks and a can of Coke. 'Thanks,' he said, and proceeded to tear open a chocolate bar wrapper.

'You eat,' she said, 'I want to say something, alright?' He nodded, chewing, an arm encircling the cache. 'You've been here a long while now. Amazing how quick ten years goes by, huh. Or maybe not.'

He gave her a wry smile, snapped open the tab on the can.

Beneath the table she pushed her knees together to stop them trembling. 'I used to hate you for what you did to our family. I wanted you to rot in prison and never feel the sun on your face again.' She said the words calmly, without aggression. His head was so low that his chin touched his chest. 'I didn't want you to live while our beautiful daughter was gone forever. It didn't seem right, didn't seem fair. My husband and I barely made it through those first years. We fought, many times but tried to stay together. In the end our hurt was bigger than our love for each other.'

She paused, thinking. The young man still didn't look up, didn't reach for his half-eaten Snickers bar. His hands were in fists on his lap, he balled them up tight, then released them.

'Why don't we just sit for a moment?' She reached for his hand, and, tentatively, he placed his in hers. He shut his eyes as she enclosed his hand with hers, as if trying to warm him through touch.

*

I want to forget where I'm from, his thoughts like a jerky video playback. *The stink of our filthy house, dirty washing up in the sink, mould on the walls, the empty vodka and whisky bottles, never having enough food, never having new clothes, never having friends over because I was too ashamed of my parents, where I lived.*

He had not received any visits until today. Just one terse note from his mother, in a generic birthday card soon after sentencing. He had opened the card and the smile had died on his lips as he read the message. He could still see it, as if were right here on the table before him.

Joe. We're ashamed to have you as our son. Don't ever come home again. Mum.

He recalled how he had felt, as though he had been punched, how he read it over and over almost masochistically, trying to sense just how much he was and always had been despised by his mother, and whether there was any love, however little, behind the scrawled three letters, 'Mum'. Even though he hadn't been close to his family, he still felt like a huge piece of him had been ripped away.

*

Meredith and Joe sat, hands touching, the hum of the room around them, sharing and not sharing their memories.

There's been a bad accident. Come to the hospital, quickly.

A young couple. Looks like a rollover. Car's a write-off for sure. He's conscious now, he'd been drinking, says he was showing off his new stereo to his girlfriend and wasn't concentrating. The road was greasy from yesterday's rain. They brought her back once, but she bled out internally and they couldn't save her in the end.

I want to see my daughter.

Are you sure?

I want to kill him. I want to die. I want to die.

'Joe,' she said, and he opened his eyes, which glistened with tears. He roughly brushed them away using his sleeve. 'I can't say I've forgiven you, not yet anyway.' *But I know I want to.* 'It's still hard for me, you know. When people ask if I have kids, and then I tell them that she died that way, and only eighteen, they don't know what to do or say.'

He nodded, and looked her squarely in the eye.

'I know you're completing your sentence soon.'

'Mm-hmm.'

'Do you know where you'll be staying?'

Shook his head. Mumbled something about a halfway house in the inner city.

'You can stay with me. In her old room. It's small, but it'll be better than nothing.'

His eyes widened.

'My brother needs an extra pair of hands. He has a gardening business. You'll be paid, and you can give me a little for the rent and board, the rest you can save.'

His mouth opened but he couldn't get a word out.

She tilted her head at him. 'Is that a yes?'

He nodded vigorously. 'I… thank you.' He dried his eyes again.

Her face lost its taut, sharp edges. 'Thank *you*,' she replied.

Band Try-outs

by Amy Mutha

Lucas tightened his grip on his guitar as he rushed to the school auditorium. He willed the nerves in his stomach to relax. It was just a school band try-out.

Of course, it was no ordinary band try-out, because Lucas didn't go to an ordinary school. Lucas was a student at the Fade Academy of Witches and Warlocks. The Fade Academy's band was nothing like an ordinary school's band. The students played magical instruments and sang spells rather than songs.

These musical spells created a low-gravity environment which was perfect for the school's dance team. The dancers were able to perform spectacular leaps and flips in the low-gravity environment.

To further enhance the performance, the artists of the school would create magical drawings which they would enchant and bring to life onstage.

One year the artists drew fierce dragons to join the dancers. The dancers gracefully leapt between the flames of the dragons to give a spectacular performance. It was much safer to animate drawings of dragons than it would have been bringing live ones onstage. Another year the artists drew a beautiful snow-covered landscape with giant dancing snowflakes and candy canes.

Every single member of the Fade Academy performing arts department was vital in putting together these phenomenal performances. Lucas wanted nothing more than to be a part of it.

But in a school full of abnormal students, Lucas was perhaps the strangest of them all. Lucas had a secret: his mother was a witch, but his father was a werewolf. Neither of Lucas's brothers had inherited his father's werewolf side, but Lucas had.

Warlocks didn't get along with werewolves, so he was sent to live in a pack with his father's family while his brothers attended the Fade Academy. One day Lucas had decided he wanted to embrace his warlock side and learn magic. Werewolves, vampires, and faeries were not allowed at Fade Academy, so Lucas kept his werewolf side a secret.

It hadn't been easy for Lucas to adjust to life among warlocks. Whenever the full moon approached he would get awfully ill. When the moon rose in the sky he would turn into a vicious animal with no memories of his human self. If he caught scent of human flesh he would want to tear it apart. But the band try-outs were the day of a full moon.

Lucas begged every member of the administration to allow him to audition on any other day, but all of his grovelling was in vain. So, he had to make a decision; should he risk it?

He always stayed far away from the school on the full moon. He didn't want his secret to be discovered, and he was terrified of hurting someone. But Lucas's passion was playing guitar, and for the first time in his life he had the chance to share his passion with others. That chance was worth risking everything for. The day came, and Lucas took a deep breath before going into the auditorium.

A boy was on the large stage playing a trumpet. The auditorium had several thick cushioned lounge chairs and a few tables where the artists could draw. The auditorium didn't have a ceiling, it opened to the skies.

In one of the chairs Lucas saw Emma Vega. She was beautiful, popular, and flunking nearly every class, but it didn't matter because she was probably the most talented magical dancer the school had ever seen.

Emma looked at Lucas as he entered the auditorium. Her perfect skin creased into a frown above her dazzling green eyes. Emma was the only student who suspected something was off about Lucas, she didn't trust him. Lucas had no idea how, or even whether, she had worked out his secret.

Lucas approached Mr Graves, the band teacher.

'Sorry I'm late–' he began.

Mr Graves pointed to an empty lounge chair at the back of the room.

When the boy finished playing his trumpet, everyone in the auditorium burst into applause.

'Up next is Rose playing the bass,' Mr Graves announced when the applause died down.

Rose is pretty good, Lucas thought.

Several people performed after her. Lucas shook his leg impatiently as he watched the performances. Finally, he went up to Mr Graves.

'Hey, can I please go next?' Lucas asked. 'I'm not feeling well so if you could please let me go next–'

Lucas was pale and sweating. Mr Graves must have noticed this because he nodded.

Lucas climbed onto the stage; his head felt like it would burst. But he hardly noticed his headache as he played his song.

When he finished, he began to retune his guitar for his next song when Mr Graves cried, 'You're in! That was an excellent performance! You are definitely lead guitar!'

'But I only played one song,' Lucas said lamely.

'And that song is all I needed to hear to know that you're the perfect lead guitarist,' Mr Graves stated matter-of-factly.

'Great, thank you so much,' said Lucas with relief as he ran off the stage, nearly bumping into a boy holding drumsticks.

As Lucas reached the exit of the auditorium someone tapped his shoulder hard. Lucas turned around and was greeted by Emma's glaring face.

'Are you stupid?' she demanded.

Lucas looked at her uncomprehendingly.

'The people who make it into the band need to stay here and perform for the dance auditions.'

Lucas's heart sank. He had completely forgotten. The only thing he wanted to do was lie in a hole and sleep until his transformation, but he couldn't jeopardize his spot in the band. Grudgingly he dragged himself back to his seat.

When the band auditions were over, everyone who made it in took their instruments to a thick silver platform at the edge of the stage, and the first dancer stepped to the centre of the stage.

Lucas nearly dropped his guitar when the thick silver platform began to levitate. He waited apprehensively for the platform to stop elevating, but this only happened when it reached about fifty feet in the air.

'What if we fall?' Lucas asked.

Mr Graves shrugged indifferently.

'Don't worry,' said Rose, the bass player. 'The platform is huge. We're far enough away from the edge all around.'

Lucas went to the edge of the platform and peered over. Rose was right. He looked down at the couches. As a werewolf, he knew he could probably survive a fifty-foot drop off the platform, so long as he landed on one of the soft cushions. Still, Lucas had always been afraid of heights.

When he started to play his guitar he forgot all his fears. He found the magical music environment incredibly soothing. He had never felt this good so close to a transformation. He played his guitar joyfully, immersing himself in the music surrounding him.

But as the band began to play the last song Lucas felt his bones begin to break. He felt the blood in his veins boil. He needed to get himself away from the people surrounding him, now. How was he going to get off the levitating platform? He took a deep breath through his nose.

'Mr Graves, I need to go to the bathroom. Can you please lower the platform?'

Mr Graves shook his head.

Lucas didn't have time to get angry; he had to act. He inched himself towards the edge of the platform and looked down at the nearest couch. He had no choice. His werewolf mind blocked out his fear.

He gave himself a bit of a running start and leapt off the platform. He landed in a crouch, not only to cushion his fall, but because his legs were starting to bend into their wolf shape.

He darted through the doors of the auditorium and out towards the thick forest that surrounded the school. If he could make it into the trees his secret would be safe and no one would get hurt.

A scream rang in his ears. Lucas's head whipped back to see Emma staring at him.

She had followed him. She had seen him transform. He watched her turn around and run back to the school.

With every ounce of willpower Lucas could muster, he managed not to chase after her.

The Pianola Player

by Mary Walter

To me he was the big brother I never had, fun, always joking, wanting to show me his latest magic trick. I had an older sister, but what good was that? She found me a pain, tagging along, whereas Gordon didn't think I was too little to bother with. He also had a younger sister and included her in all we did. Whenever we visited, we cousins were left to our own devices in their big house; while our parents disappeared to the kitchen, we raced from room to room.

We played Cheat – I couldn't help blushing so everyone knew when I was cheating. Gordon showed me card games and tricks; he showed me Patience and Clock Patience, how to deal and how to slide the cards spectacularly from one hand to the other. He was so clever, what made him choose his strange path?

He 'played' to us on the pianola, and because I knew he and my sister had piano lessons together he fooled me completely. I came into the room, entranced by his rendition of a Chopin nocturne that I knew from my mother's repertoire. Then I was shocked as he removed his hands from the keyboard and waved them in the air! He laughed at my astonished face as the keys went on playing by themselves.

Perhaps that was the only time he and my sister shared a joke at my expense. It was only a joke, but later Gordon lived his life like that, a life of pretence.

The pianola and the billiard table were in the Map Room. There were antique maps of London hanging huge and brown on every wall. I would stand before them, trying to make them out. I could recognise the Thames in yellowing blue, dividing north and south.

We were not allowed to touch the green baize table in the centre of the room, with its brightly coloured balls that made such a satisfying click when they hit one another. We tried playing – Gordon replaced all the balls correctly so no one would know. We realised it was a sly thing to do but it wasn't till later that his scheming assumed greater significance.

Upstairs there was a room they called the Box Room. This wasn't the customary small room but was where they stored boxes. We used to duck in and out of them, playing chase and hide-and-seek. I was told they were full of the *Daily Worker* newspapers Gordon's parents distributed but I didn't know what that meant. The mysterious, rather sinister brown boxes loomed over me as I darted between them in the dim light.

Gordon told us that their house was haunted and I wanted to see the ghost, but my sister was sceptical. Gordon said he would show us. That evening he took us down the Secret Tunnel. He told us to be absolutely quiet as it was strictly forbidden. The four of us picked our way silently along with a fearful fascination, through the rubbish and the builders' debris in the pitch dark beneath the house.

Gordon was leading the way at the front, shining the torch ahead. Suddenly he swung round, shining the beam in our eyes with a ghostly 'WOOOH!' I screamed and Gordon's father came rushing downstairs. He told us our tunnel was just a prosaic basement and very dangerous. 'Don't you ever go down there again!' he threatened his son. I suppose, looking back, it was clear that Gordon liked doing things he shouldn't.

But the day we went to the fair, no one got into trouble: it was all rides and fairylights, candyfloss and delight. Elatedly, I hooked a duck from the pool and won a comb – which was less fun than the hooking, so Gordon shouldered a rifle and presented me with a plaster dog. Our fathers competed to hit the bell at the top of the post, with a hammer far too heavy for them, and then we all swung on the swing-boats and dodged on the dodgems. On the way home, Gordon was making everyone laugh; he made me feel the centre of attention, instead of, as the youngest, having no one listen to me.

Later, as a young man, he had not neglected us. He would call in every holiday with his fiancée, on his way home from their northern university, playing the piano for us. He taught me tunes, contemporary pop songs, that I can still play to this day: 'Answer Me', 'Because', 'Happy Birthday Sweet Sixteen'….

When I grew up and visited him with my husband, he made a friend of him too. 'Let me show you this, it's really fancy!' Gordon would say, full of his characteristic enthusiasm. He rushed off to show us his latest gadget, from digital clocks and Rubik's cubes of the 1970s to the state-of-the-art Apple Mac forty years later that he'd got for such a bargain. He gave us rides in his BMW – 'Slow down, Gordon, slow down!' shrilled his wife. We pored over the photos of his business trip to Thailand. 'Marvellous service, order anything you want, champagne and caviar, whatever, you know, *whatever*!' He gave us a mischievous look and we laughed uneasily.

'Play us something,' I implored him, as on all our visits, and he played me, 'I Will Survive', singing with a heart-rending break in his voice.

And then the bombshell hit us. I could hardly take in the story, accept it as being about the Gordon I knew. His wife rang us one summer evening and told us how the police had arrived and taken her husband away. Her life, her family's lives, had changed forever, and I had to review our friendship. Over the following months she filled in more and more of the horrid details, but we never visited him. 'Answer Me', I played on our piano, wondering if he could.

When he was released on licence three years later, he gave us 'his side of the story'. We sat dumbly in our sitting room, my husband and I on the sofa, looking across an abyss at Gordon in the armchair opposite. He had left us and gone over to a dark way of life. His 'explanations' made no sense to us, conventionally married as we were.

His wife had moved to an undisclosed address and their divorce was in progress. His two sons would no longer speak to him, protective of their teenage daughters. Only his sister still looked out for him and he now lived near her. He had had to give up his beautiful house whose garden he had tended so carefully, through all the time of living a Jekyll and Hyde existence.

'My mother *loved* Gordon,' said his white-faced wife, 'Thank goodness she never lived to know.'

The family debated endlessly what motive he could have had for his bizarre behaviour – he and his wife got on well, didn't they? They were always teasing each other.

'We should have guessed what was coming, from what he was like as a boy,' nodded the aged aunt sagely, recalling an occasion when he had helped himself to four chocolate biscuits all at once.

'I guess life brings many changes,' wrote his elderly half-brother philosophically from Canada. But to us it was like staring at the unseen face of the moon.

Was there any way back to family affection and acceptance? When he arrived he looked the same, though rather the worse for wear, charming and chatty as always, but knowledge spoiled the picture and removed the veils through which we usually see our friends. He sat facing us, confidently confessing all, sometimes appearing rueful, but somehow not really sorry.

'I had "enhanced" status,' he boasted, 'That meant I had privileges, I could go outside and walk about the grounds, not like the IPP prisoners. All one chap had done was smack a girl's bottom.' He drank a mouthful of wine, then added in a matter of fact way, 'He can't prove he won't do it again and so he'll never get out.'

Trying for connection with the Gordon of old I enquired, 'Keeping up your music?'

'Can't,' he explained. 'No piano now and choirs all perform in the evenings – I'm on curfew.' He added, entirely characteristically, 'So I go to church and sing the hymns.'

He spoke in the same familiar north London accent I had been brought up with and rarely heard now I lived in the West Country. In that warm voice I thought for a moment I had found again the real Gordon. How could I give him up? The memories of our shared childhood were too dear to me.

We kissed cheeks as usual on parting, but our embrace did not cross the divide. He had not even had time to play the piano for me. Painfully I came to realise that there was no meeting place left for us – except in the past.

Every Breath You Take

by Mike Evis

Helen knew her daughter had put *that* ringtone on her phone deliberately to annoy her. Typical teenager. 'Can't you choose something else?' she said, after Anna's phone rang for the fifth time in ten minutes. As if she didn't hear that song enough at work.

'What's it to you?' said Anna, slamming the door. Helen used to like The Police, but lately 'Every Breath You Take' was getting on her nerves. The song seemed to be speaking directly to her, taunting her, as did 'Roxanne', the other Police track used in the backing music for her routine. Why had they replaced the clubbing music with a string of '70s and '80s hits?

'Shouldn't worry, love,' said Jerry, puffing a fag as he stood, hands on hips, eyes glued to her cleavage. 'The punters don't care how well you dance. They just want to see–'

'Look, can't you change some of the tracks?' she said.

He shook his head, without shifting his gaze for a second. 'No can do. Estelle, love, it's what they want.' And she wondered – could it be him? Could he be the one behind it?

'Come on, you know what they're like. Load of old tossers

in their fifties. It's their music, innit?'

It was true. All those sad men in suits, the sadder ones in stained pullovers and T-shirts, their tongues hanging out, all those leering faces – you could hardly avoid feeling sheer contempt. Every night, facing the audience, she put up that glass barrier in her head as she climbed the pole, the music pounding, trying not to wince when 'Every Breath You Take' started.

'Get 'em off, love.'

'Show us your–'

She treated them to her finest look of disdain, making it perfectly clear who was being demeaned here. Sometimes they'd try to touch her, or put their business cards in her tips glass. 'What you doing afterwards, love?' they'd call, and she'd give a contemptuous curl of her lip. As if she would descend to their level. They were nothing more than drooling beasts.

After a few months on the job, she learned that really it was she who was in charge. But, overnight, her confidence had been shaken. The email looked like spam and she nearly deleted it, before realising it wasn't junk at all.

So tonight, as she walked across the deserted city centre square leading to the Half Moon Inn, her heels clicking noisily on the concrete, she was far from in control. Behind the façade – her hair scraped back into a pony tail, the layers of make-up, the kohl round her eyes – she was apprehensive. She'd feared something like this when she first started dancing, but as time went by she became blasé. It would never happen – but now it had.

She paused at the entrance to the alleyway, wondering if she was being foolish. Surely there could be nothing in this? Just some chancer. She shivered.

'Hello Estelle,' the email began. 'You don't know me, but I know all about you and your dirty little secret. And it isn't Estelle, is it? It's Helen.'

She'd looked away from the screen in shock. How could anyone know? How had he – for it must be a he – found out? And what would she do if he started telling people? How would she face the other mums at Anna's school? Would parents tell their children to keep away from Anna from now on?

Endlessly, she read the email over, poring over the words, trying to squeeze meaning from each phrase.

'You act so high and mighty. But we know you're just a–'
When she read that, she had to glance away.

'Let's come to an arrangement.'

Did he mean a financial arrangement – or something else?

'Meet me at the Half Moon Inn on Tuesday. I know that's your night off. I'll be sitting in the corner. Unless you want everyone to know.'

So here she was. She'd managed to compose herself in the quiet and solitude of the square, but now her reserves of calm began to evaporate. And as she got closer she could hear 'Every Breath You Take' blaring out from behind the steamed-up windows. She wanted to believe it was coincidence, but was it? Why was she hearing it everywhere she went? Everything blurred into a fuzzy mess in her head. She stood, frozen, waiting for the song to finish.

*

'So,' she demanded, standing at the table, hands on hips, her expression tens of degrees below zero, 'What was it you had in mind?'

He looked confused. She was just as puzzled – he didn't look the type to visit the club, let alone attempt blackmail.

Young, twenties perhaps, a wispy beard, John Lennon glasses, and slightly built. A geek.

'I– I–' he stammered, taking his glasses off, fiddling with his half pint. 'I thought a chat, that's – that's all.'

The ice in her glare melted. She could eat him for breakfast. Yet, men – weren't they all the same under the skin? She was careful not to relax; she couldn't afford to let her guard down.

When she'd walked in, after pausing to neaten up her pony tail and ensure she had the right cold look on her face, she saw there was only one table in the corner with a single person – a man – sitting at it. It had to be him. She'd taken a deep breath, and strode deliberately to his table, letting him take the full measure of her heels, her stockinged legs. She was ready, even if she felt a tremor inside. The trick was not to show it.

'You don't look like your photo,' he said now, as she took a seat.

She felt a flash of anger. Had this geek taken pictures in the club?

'They don't allow photos,' she said.

Sipping his beer, he looked confused. She wondered what he would ask for. He looked so timid. With luck, perhaps she could play it so whatever he asked for wasn't too bad.

She was prepared. In the club she was constantly propositioned: hands would grope her bottom, pieces of paper with phone numbers would be slipped into her hand, businessmen would announce, 'I'm staying at the Hilton – want to drop by later?' It was so mind-numbingly predictable – like her act. You just climbed up and down the pole a few times, showed them some bare flesh, and that was it.

She motioned towards his empty glass. Might as well get a drink out of this. 'Aren't you going to get me one, then?' she said. He actually blushed. *He's so young*, she thought.

'Mine's a vodka and lime,' she said, smiling at him.

Jarring the table, he got up. Surely a chat couldn't be all he was after?

When he returned with her drink he nearly spilled it. *Poor lamb*, she thought, *he's nervous*. She caught herself. *No sympathy, not after that email.*

Then she heard the first few chords of 'Roxanne' playing from the jukebox and any remnants of sympathy vanished. He must have put it on when he went to the bar. With its talk of red lights and walking the streets, the white heat of anger rose within her.

'You don't have to rub it in,' she said.

'Rub what in?'

'You know, the music. Whatever you want–'

'I only thought we should get to know each other.'

'Surely you already know all there is to know,' she said, leaning on her elbow. 'Your email–'

In her handbag, her phone started to faintly play the first bar of 'Every breath You Take'. Anna's idea of a joke, she supposed, setting it as the ringtone on her mum's phone too. She decided to ignore the call. Probably the club wanting her to come in on her night off. There were always girls not showing up.

'There's only so much you can write.' He shrugged. 'So, what made you go in for this?'

'Why do you think? I'm a single mum.'

'Oh, you didn't mention you had a child,' he said. 'I guess that makes it hard to meet people.'

She nodded.

'Let's discuss what we're looking for,' he said, not meeting her eye.

Oh God, she thought, *this is it. What will he ask for? Something kinky, degrading – or just money? I don't know which would be worse.*

'If it's money–'

'Money? What's that got to do with it?'

This is what I feared, she thought.

'What I want is a relationship. I thought I explained that.'

'Sweetheart,' she said, speaking very slowly, 'that's not–'

An agitated young woman was standing at their table.

'You Kevin?' she said. 'You could've told me you'd found another date. Half an hour I've been sat here, wasting my time, and here you are with some other woman. Well, forget it.'

'You're–'

'Susan.'

'But I thought–'

Helen reached down for her phone. There were two messages.

'Where are you?'

followed by

'Are you taking the mickey, chatting up some other bloke? Our deal's off. Your dirty little secret is coming out.'

'Every Breath You Take' began to play again over the speakers.

Baker's Practical Segue

by Matthew C. McLean

The pentagram was correct, the symbols along its border perfect. Dee had double checked each facet of the summoning circle seven times, once with the computer's scanner, making sure everything was in place. The salt made a mess on the Persian rug, but he'd clean it up later and, if he couldn't, it was worth the price.

The ritual had to be performed in the perfect privacy that only his penthouse could afford. Otherwise, his public might find out his secret, and the ideal life he had carved out for himself would come to an end.

Satisfied with the fidelity of the protective circle he smiled and walked to the piano. Sitting on the bench he adjusted the small audio player on the grand's top board, then selected the play button. The ethereal voices of a cantata came forth from the box's speakers and Dee took a moment to enjoy the high sweetness before he laid his fingers on the ivory keys. Like the voices, his accompaniment started out slow and light, but progressed at an increasing rhythm. His hands moved further and further towards the bass keys of the piano as the voices became higher, more strained and tortured, as if victim to the music itself.

The dissonance between recording and piano continued until it seemed to drain the light from the room itself, darkness enfolding player and piano, swirling out to occupy greater space until the crescendo mounted to its zenith. If anyone had been present there would have been nothing for them to see at the ending notes, the room cloaked in blackness.

With a concluding striking chord, the darkness dissipated with a speed that belied its slow arrival. And standing in the pentagram where no man had been before stood a grey and tired figure, what might have been a young man, in tattered clothes holding a simple guitar, an itinerant in this life and the next. He kept his hat on his head, shading his eyes from the room's central chandelier, and frowned a, 'Hello Dee.'

'Hello Baker. Feeling rested I hope?'

The grey around the spirit called Baker darkened into a shadow that poured down his body from the brim of his hat. 'What do you want, Dee?'

'Good news! I've been invited to the royal wedding. They've asked me to bring a new composition to the reception. I need something light and catchy.'

The shadows around Baker darkened until he appeared as an onyx figure. 'You know the kind of pain it causes me for you to bring me back into this space. And you want me to make you some ear-candy?'

'As only you can.' Dee arched his thin fingers together. 'Preferably with some lyrics about eternal love.'

Baker shifted, holding his guitar by the neck as if it were a club. 'My take on eternity is a little different these days.'

Dee used the temple of his fingers to point at the spirit he had called upon as if it were a petulant child. 'Don't be so grim.'

'You bring me back here to write songs for you, making yourself rich off a talent that never got me recognition in life.' Baker's eyes burned through his shadow. 'And your advice is to "lighten up"?'

Dee smiled, splaying his fingers, indicating an obvious conclusion. 'Indeed. It's not as if you have a choice.'

Baker stood, moments passing and the dark shadow around him fading slightly. 'Maybe you should try asking Michael. I heard he was working up tunes for the Heavenly Choir.'

Dee frowned his disapproval. 'You know I can't bring up anyone with a recognisable style.'

'So you need someone who died in anonymity.'

Clapping, Dee spoke fawningly, 'But a genius who died in anonymity!'

The shadow and his resolve drained away, Baker slowly responded, '...Thanks.' He shifted the guitar he carried into both hands, cradling it. 'Could I at least get a stool?'

Dee gave a laugh that was famous in the media, a laugh some privately thought carried a tone of menace. 'That's almost clever, Baker. You know I can't break the circle.'

Baker gave the guitar a strum. 'Or I'll escape.'

Tilting his bald head, Dee smiled pityingly. 'You escaping is not what I'm worried about. There's always another unsung talent in the Great Beyond I can call on.'

'You're worried about what I'd do to you if I got out,' Baker smiled.

Dee returned the grin. 'I'm so glad we understand each other.'

'I'm not a killer, Dee. Never have been.'

'Pardon me if I don't take that chance.' Running a finger along his scalp, the necromancer turned to leave. 'Now get to work. The sooner you're done the sooner I'll put you back.' Dee checked his watch, the anachronistic time piece so bejewelled it might have been the reason they invented the word 'bling'. 'How long will you need?'

Baker tuned his guitar, looking down the struts, pointing the instrument's neck at his summoner like a gun sight. 'Not long. I've got something I had been working on that no one's ever heard. I can rework it pretty quickly.'

Dee smiled with approval. 'I'll be back in an hour.' And in an hour he returned, sitting on the piano's bench with a patient smile. 'So, what do you have for me?'

Baker didn't reply, but instead began to play a song. It didn't sound to Dee like what he had asked for, not some light pop tune, but a wilder strain of notes. It so struck the necromancer that he began to play it out on the grand when Baker came back to the chorus a second time.

Dee felt the music move into a shifting etherealness that carried him through several more rounds of music. Accompanying the guitarist, he asked, 'This is... unusual. Does it need percussion?'

'No.' The response caused Dee to jump, the music broken by his hands banging the piano keys. Baker hadn't spoken.

Glaring behind him, Dee saw another grey figure, a bearded and bald man in an ancient tunic with a flaring white ruff around the neck. His eyes burned with a fire not dissimilar to what Dee had seen in Baker shortly before. The man's rigid posture held him taut like a string ready to snap.

'I'm happy to disappoint you, Dee.' Baker spoke from what seemed a great distance away. 'The tune isn't mine. I learned it from one of the Utom people on the other side. They're South American forest dwellers who speak to their ancestors through music. To be specific,' Baker concluded, 'they use that tune to summon the dead, but without circles or other components.'

Dee eyed the man standing next to him. 'This is…?'

'Oh, no.' Dee could hear laughter in Baker's voice. 'He's not Utom. This is Carlo Gesualdo da Venosa. He's a Count and composer from sixteenth-century Italy.' Baker paused, then added, 'He also tortured and murdered his wife and her lover.'

'He's got a thing about personal property. So I asked him to come up here and have a chat with you about stealing other people's work.'

Notes, Surrounded

by Colin Heaney

There was music in life. Paul could sense it, the pulsating beats and irregular rhythms of it all. It was sectioned and cordoned off, like the herds on the great meadows.

What was the music like along the thoroughfare? Or in the living room? Or out and beyond to sea, where the waves crashed and thrashed and beat their loud, heavy drums on the soil of reality? It was ever-flowing and evanescent. It was truth and lies and justice and betrayal holding hands and pressing their sweaty palms together.

But to Paul the worst notes came from his workplace, from the office with its buzzing fluorescent lights and cooling fans, lightly fluttering pages, with an occasional snicker only matched by someone's guttural cough.

Paul despised his environment. It was his rudimentary cave, and the computer and papers before him his primitive tools. The illumined screen shot needles into his eyes, wedging deep into his mind and disrupting the pitch of his own, personal music, so the cooling electric fan became a destructive hurricane and the coughs from his colleagues world-shattering earthquakes.

He wanted out. He wanted to breathe the fresh air and listen to the beeps of cars, he wanted to explore the forests and the local lakes, he wanted to turn his ear towards the swishing and swashing blue canvas and the caressing wind as it travelled untethered above.

But Paul was not the wind. He was only poison to the atmosphere – a fossil-burning human tethered to life, all its burdens weighing on him like revelations of cosmic importance.

Footsteps came towards him. Click. Pause. Click. Pause. Click. Stop.

The shiny leather shoes acted as a mirror and a face, and as Mr Murr spoke he imagined the shoes addressing him. They said:

'Paul. You've only got sections A to B2 filed. You were supposed to be moving on to C. I'm afraid you're going to have to work the weekend. Here are the rest of the specifications.'

Mr Murr rested the page on the desk and swiftly made off to his own corner office, cushy and inviting in contrast to the sterile bleakness of the mass of cubicles.

Paul ignored the specifications. He half-raised himself from his cubicle and peered around at the other animals in the zoo. They were all in their cages, creating music. The keyboards clicked, the printers roared, someone sighed, then the pattern repeated itself. Click. Roar. Sigh. Click. Roar. Sigh.

Paul could only see heads across the drab, grey landscape, some bald, others adorned with hair. They all faced screens and pages, pages and screens. This was it. This was his life. An ambience of slow dissipation ended each day, only for a return to the metallic creaks of his mouldy home, and his frail wife, her shrill complaints acting as lyrics to accompany it all:

'You lack drive, Paul. You lack ambition. You're a drifter.'

No, Paul thought. *I am a listener, and the attentive ear prevails. I am the quiet one in the concert hall, sipping his drink in a languid manner and gently swaying. I won't embrace life*, he determined, *and in turn it won't embrace me.*

But in the end Paul could stand it no longer. The mind-numbing consistency of it all: the office and its rules, his wife and her lamentations, society and its judgements.

He rose to his feet in his cubicle, spilling a container of pens across the specifications, the pages blown on their way by the electric fan.

'Goodbye,' Paul whispered to no one in particular, before making his way to the elevator.

He heard Mr Murr stirring, rising, then releasing a torrent of orders:

'Get back here, Paul! What do you think you're doing? I'll have you on the streets for this. Do you hear me?'

Of course Paul heard. Paul heard everything. He heard the gentle piano musak playing in the elevator and the groans of the sliding doors opening. He heard clusters of people talking and laughing in the lobby, a woman discussing the recent natural disaster while a man smiled and sympathised. Then he heard the man on reception saying his greetings as Paul bid him adieu.

He was outside and the din was excessive, crazy. There was happiness here, and anger, and love, and hate, and all the little emotions between. They were all here, and Paul's life was building to a great crescendo. He could feel it, and he knew what he had to do. He would stroll down the pavement, say hello to passers-by, wave, smile, incline his head, get a coffee, then keep walking. He'd find a bench and sit. He'd allow life to wash over him, as if a soothing showerhead hovered above him, rinsing off his worries.

For the first time, he was going to enjoy the music. He was going to shut his eyes and embrace it.

This was it, he thought. The greatest concert in the world.

Wagner in the Marsh

by David Hamilton

They spooked me when I was thirteen, with music. I don't believe they did it deliberately and at the time I didn't see it as getting spooked.

Form III of my Exeter school had gone on this junket to Norfolk. We were guests of a grand house in a village east of Norwich. One evening they showed us a video shot by locals, about the area and its history. The video had accompanying music which immediately startled me so much that I burst out, 'That music's *fantastic.*'

You can imagine the reactions of my leg-pulling classmates. I provoked enough uproar to make the kindly supervisors pause the video.

'Alan, isn't it? How is the music grabbing you?'

'It's the *style* of it. It stirs and – and – *carries* you and keeps throwing in sort of – tone changes you don't expect and which sort of *tingle* you....'

'In his own way,' the teacher said to the group, 'Alan is quite articulate. He's certainly not the first to perceive that in many ways Richard Wagner's music is unique. Without wishing to offend you, Alan, I'll guess the only non-pop tune you can name is "God Save The Queen"? Well, the music that's impressed you is called "Morning and Siegfried's Rhine Journey", it's the prologue to Wagner's opera, *Gotterdammerung*. We'll look into feeding your interest, Alan, if in the meantime you'll bear with us and enjoy the rest of the video?'

The next morning we hiked into nearby marshland. Before we started out, Mr Donald Dunn, a hugely likeable and good-natured gentleman, and our main host, buttonholed me.

During a long stare down at me from kindly blue eyes he said, 'My daughter's lending you this, Alan. Just a small pack in your pocket – so – and a wire to the earpiece, and Wagner can entertain you while you walk, without bothering anyone else.'

The marsh was fairyland. A vast flatness in myriad shades, every shade distinctly individual, the predominant greens glowing luminous, a distant straight road with tiny vehicles seeming at a higher level than we were. The fairies had upturned a huge bowl over it all, after painting the vessel an enchanting azure and cutting a hole to let a golden sun flood in. Silver glints abounded, edged by the strange, stark beauty of Norfolk reeds.

There were ditches, and broader cuts through the flatness called dykes, their water level subtly higher and easing away to be pumped into high-banked rivers to the sea: roughly, that's how land drainage works. We entered the vista with the prologue to *Gotterdammerung* in my ear, and, somehow, nuances in the sounds matched what my eyes were seeing.

We came upon this strange structure. Like several distant others, it was a truncated cone. About ten metres high and six in diameter of base, brick-built, now a crumbling shell. A defunct windmill, you might think, with two remaining skeletons of sails. No, the video had told us it used to be a wind*pump*, built in bygone years under the supervision of imported Hollanders, who knew a bit about land drainage and must have left countless descendants in East Norfolk plus many words in its dialect. For instance, in East Norfolk a cloth for wiping the floor is called a dwile – and it's the same word for the same thing in The Netherlands.

Despite being derelict, abandoned and forgotten, the windpump had dignity and eerie beauty. The music in my ear changed as I stared at it, to a rapid tattoo suggesting drums without sounding them.

Evading supervision, I achieved a dangerous climb inside. At the top, the bird's-eye view of horizon-to-horizon green flatness was superb. Spellbound, I found I could let my imagination ramble gloriously. I was king, conquering General, all-wise sage, powerful and unchallengeable, while in my ear the music slowed, teasingly, hinting partnership with my imaginings.

A shout drifted, 'Alan, stay still.' It was Donald Dunn, far below. 'A rope will be thrown up, Alan. Let it rest on brickwork behind you. Remember the bowline knot we learned? Put yourself in a bowline on a bight, after taking off your jacket to pad your armpits. We'll gradually pay out the rope, taking your weight as you climb down. Stay calm, shout when ready.'

I achieved the final couple of metres as the music gathered, trumpets swelling into an eerily thrilling zenith. Mr Dunn leaned close to listen too, his blue eyes searching my face as he untied the rope. 'Siegfried has gone instead of you, thank God,' he said. 'That was his funeral music.' He stared into the distance, then added, 'You'll be back here one day, I think.'

When our stay ended, Mr Dunn's daughter, an enchanting early-twenties blonde, shook her head. 'Keep the player, Alan. With *Gotterdammerung* in your ear, you'll be prompted to learn far more than pop could teach you.'

Back home in Devon, Wagner's music stayed with me, growing up, and, because it stayed, that Norfolk village and the marsh around it remained strong in my memory too.

Somehow, even when unbidden by audio gadgets, the music played in my head to mark significant moments. I passed GCSE exams to *Siegfried Idyll*, achieved A-levels to *Tannhauser Overture*, my grandmother died peacefully to *Parsifal*, and I graduated from university with *Die Meistersingers*.

Relaxing at home after graduating, I happened upon family lore. Hazy, even non-confirmable though it was, the implication was that my great-grandfather and his wife had hailed from that very Norfolk village where I had acquired Wagner, and had regarded their move to Devon as unwanted exile. The great-grandfather had launched a family business we had inherited, and which had recently been sold with resulting financial benefit to me. Perhaps inevitably, I romanticised. Had my great-grandfather intended that one day, one of his descendants would have the financial ease to return for him to Reedby-in-the-Marsh?

Well, I reasoned, the work I now want to take up can be done on a computer from any base, so why not make Reedby my base?

Locals here are now nonplussed by a young man who arrived to settle because, he freely admits, he *feels in his bones* his heritage is here. Heritage should be an easily definable word, but they conclude that I, Alan Myhill, have invaded their heritage as a result of a personal mysticism.

They rib me about it. However, they do nod thoughtfully if someone notices that my West Country burr is already acquiring hints of their guttural, heavy consonants and lingering-vowelled Norfolk accent.

The Dunn family still live here, Donald Dunn and his daughter, and I recall their roots have been in Reedby for countless generations. They remember me, are impeccably civil, and do not rib me. Mr Dunn stares at me thoughtfully instead.

That ancient structure I climbed is called Reedby Dyke Windpump. It once lifted marsh water into Reedby Dyke, which in turn was pumped into the Yare and away to the North Sea. They have stations with electric-driven pumps now, of course.

I go to the derelict windpump often, a three-mile hike. It's difficult climbing, now I'm bigger. At the top, the wind slams me, roaring its desolation. Hail lashes spite. In my head, sonorous strains begin, swelling with storm-assisted force into 'Siegfried's Funeral Music'.

My boot knocks rotted wood from a box discarded inside the windpump, its lid shatters into chips, revealing papers within. An old newspaper, the *East Norfolk Herald*. No pages can be turned, it's just a wad of pulp, but on the underside I can discern a faint paragraph heading, reading 'Inquest on Reedby Dyke Tragedy'.

Wait. Amid soggy-crumbled wood is dirty yellow oilskin. I rip it apart. An envelope, yellowed but dry. I fumble and take out a sheet. Handwriting, the ink unfaded, as if written yesterday.

On this marsh where my son Desmond died, I attest to posterity. I claim, although the inquest recorded Accidental

Death, that George Myhill's departure from Reedby reflects his guilt concerning Desmond's fall from the top of Reedby Dyke Windpump. I say my claim is reinforced by another departure from Reedby, that of Desmond's sweetheart Violet Hurrel. Desmond suspected she had found another love. Why else is she gone, if not to join George Myhill?
Helen Dunn, 21st January 1919

I sway precariously, anchored only by my grasp on a rotting beam. Trumpets in my head soar to their eerily thrilling zenith, seeming to cause the sudden crumbling of the beam. My lower torso is left pressed on brickwork, my chest and head hang outside the cone, my eyes stare at the ground far below.

I feel a strong hand grasp my anorak. I cannot fall while it holds. Behind me a wind-buffeted voice says, 'Followed you. I've just read it. Incredible, but the fact is I always sensed you had baggage. She was wrong, it was later confirmed George Myhill was in Norwich at the time. He was ostracised unjustly.'

I am pulled inside the cone to safety. My head plays the finale of *Gotterdammerung*, gentler music but engagingly insisting its themes and chord-changes.

'Thanks, Mr Dunn,' I say.

'Call me Donald, now you're grown up.'

The Piano

by Camilla Johansson

The first time Alice heard the music she cried. It not only filled her rather tiny flat, but it felt like it entered every cell of her being, her soul even. It seeped down from the apartment just above hers: floating, dreamy notes from a piano, a piece she had never heard before.

After a while, she started to look forward to the morning concertos that gave her the energy she needed to get through the day, and the calmer evening sonatas that lulled her to sleep. Curious about who the talented pianist was, she one day took the stairs to the next floor and rang the doorbell, prepared to pay compliments and thank the unknown virtuoso for the beautiful music.

The tune, reminding her of an early summer morning, came to an abrupt halt as the doorbell cracked the calm like a stone in a still pond, but nothing else happened. Alice planted a determined finger on the bell and rang again, allowing it to ring for a moment longer than would typically have been considered polite. She waited.

Nothing.

She pressed her ear against the door and held her breath to

better catch any movement on the other side. Was there a sound? She pictured the occupant of the flat pressing their own ear against the inside of the same door.

Alice felt a throbbing in her ear and imagined it slowly turning red. She giggled soundlessly, visualising herself walking down the street with differently coloured ears. The giggle threatened to grow into a peel of laughter as her thoughts drifted to what would happen if whoever was in the flat flung the door open as she was standing there.

'I just want to say hello,' she whispered against the dark wood, 'and thank you for the beautiful music. I'm not here to complain.'

All the door, and the inhabitant within, offered up was silence. But behind her she could hear someone coming down the old marble stairs that connected the floors in the former Victorian townhouse.

She turned around to meet the part-curious and part-disapproving gaze of Mrs Andrews, the oldest inhabitant of the house, both in age and in years as a tenant.

'What on earth are you doing?' Mrs Andrews squinted at her as if trying to focus properly.

'I just popped up to thank whoever lives here for the lovely piano concertos he or she plays every day. Haven't you heard it, Mrs Andrews? It must be a professional pianist. I heard the music when I left my flat, but now no one wants to open the door.'

Mrs Andrews managed to muster an even more disapproving frown, and the little hat that was balancing on top of her grey hair shivered with indignation.

'Don't be ridiculous,' Mrs Andrews spat. 'No one has lived in that flat for at least a year, and no one is living there now.'

Without giving Alice a chance to react to this statement, the elderly woman continued down the next flight of stairs as fast as her weak legs could carry her. Alice found herself standing outside the closed door and silent flat not knowing what to think. Of course, someone had to be living there. Mrs Andrews was wrong.

Over the following days, finding out who was living in the flat above her became an obsession with Alice. She lost track of the number of times she called the landlord, only to be put on hold with no one ever answering, or to reach an answering machine where she was told to leave her name and number, and someone would get back to her. No one ever did.

Eventually, she turned to Google, scanning sites which claimed to at least give an idea of who lived where. She found herself, but to her dismay, the website confirmed Mrs Andrews' claim: the flat above hers seemed to be empty. Would a squatter bring a piano? Not very likely.

But the music continued. Slowly it began to frighten her.

'You do realise you must be dreaming. I bet you hear the music just as you're waking up or as you're falling asleep?' Alice's best friend and colleague Petra said, after Alice had finally decided that she needed to talk to someone about her odd experiences. Practical as ever, Petra was convinced it was all in Alice's head, an aural illusion.

'No, I'm not dreaming. I hear it when I get ready for work, when I'm preparing dinner. Someone is in that flat, playing the piano.' Alice waved her hand as Petra made another attempt to explain it away.

The truth was that Alice wished Petra was right. It would have made it easier to accept the notes that kept drifting through her ceiling with undiminished regularity.

Finally, the landlord called back, and, rattled by the possibility, even if remote, that a squatter actually had managed to drag a piano into the empty flat, he arrived at the house the very same evening, and even let Alice accompany him up to the next floor. Maybe he was afraid.

Afterwards, Alice wished that she hadn't gone up there. Not because of anything she saw, but for all the things she didn't see. As soon as Mr Richards, the landlord, opened the door, it became clear that no one was living there. The air in the rooms was stale due to lack of circulation, and not only was there no piano in sight, there was no furniture in the flat at all: no cupboard that might conceal an electric keyboard, no record player or sound system.

'Maybe you've been dreaming?' Mr Richards didn't seem worried about his flat anymore, the expression on his face indicated he was more worried about Alice.

'Yes, yes it must have been the same dream over and over again.' Alice hoped she managed to keep the sarcastic tone to a minimum as she turned around and went down to her flat without waiting for Mr Richards.

As soon as Alice, emotionally exhausted, sat down on her sofa, the music started again. She ran to the window, hoping to catch the landlord, but she only caught a glimpse of his car as he vanished into the peak-hour traffic.

Above her head, the piano player, in contrast to previous times, worked the music up to a crescendo. Then there was silence.

Alice held her breath. Was it finally over? But it started again and, for the first time, it was a melody she recognised. In the dark, empty flat on the second floor, someone started playing a melody all too familiar to her: 'Living Next Door to Alice'.

She couldn't stay there anymore. The music that she had formerly appreciated and even looked forward to hearing had turned into a nightmare.

She opened her door and ran down the street. One thing she knew: she couldn't stay in her home anymore.

The High Note

by Abby Luby

The cello was propped up in the corner of the room, strings facing inward, as I stared at its familiar arched back of deep hued mahogany and whimsical flanged markings. The instrument had been mine since I was a teenager and years of study had taught me how to make it sing.

It had been months since I had released it from its case, months that I had been paralysed by its silence. I was unwilling to sweep the bow across the strings and feel the buzz under my fingers, creating tones that resonated in my blood and out into the atmosphere. Ever since I performed for the revered Hungarian cellist János Starker here at Indiana University, I hadn't touched the cello.

At the end of each semester students were graded on a performance before the acclaimed 'maestros' at the college. These performance exams were called juries. I knew playing for Starker would be humbling and thrilling at the same time, and I plunged into endless hours of practice, as did every student at the esteemed music school.

Three floors of practice rooms in the circular music building on the Bloomington campus were always occupied, as we sacrificed eating and sleeping to feed our obsession with a flawless performance. The place buzzed like a honeycomb. Students reworked difficult passages, securing the notes in muscle memory to achieve total accuracy, and strenuously hammered out melodious cadenzas – more tactile gymnastics than lovely solos.

Was this any way to live? Even as a young cellist in high school I knew a musician's life was tough and nerve-racking. But without the cello, life was empty. Music invigorated, impassioned me. There was always a melody playing in my head, like a friend lightly skipping alongside me everywhere I went.

At Indiana, the competition among music students was fierce, and an undercurrent of one-upmanship flooded the collective psyche. We all quietly acknowledged this to ourselves but rarely to each other, unless something terrible happened.

And something terrible did happen.

A promising young vocal student had been rejected after she auditioned for a leading soprano role in an opera. Performing on the school's stage in the famous 'Big Mac' opera house (then the biggest venue between New York and California) usually guaranteed a student's future success, but not in this case. The day after her doomed audition she leapt off the roof of the music building and plunged to her death. The musical rotunda became a spiral of silence as floor by floor students realised what had happened, horror spreading upwards like an intravenous drip of numbing fluid. A few days later a lone oboe could be heard practising. Life went on.

My cello teacher, an accomplished student of János Starker, was as nervous as I was as the day of the jury approached.

His teaching skills would be judged accordingly. 'Practise! Practise!' he urged me. 'Learn all twelve scales by heart! Maestro must hear three perfect octaves!' I despised the monotonous sequence up and down the fingerboard, it made my brain freeze. I hardly ever practised scales. I would wing it.

I lacked the confidence to play a fast, flashy piece, so I chose 'Lamento', a slow solo movement written by the twentieth-century British composer Benjamin Britten. I was drawn to the solo's edgy tonalities and how its musical arc started with a soft passage, a halting and slow plaintive song that intensified, finally reaching a long held high note, ringing in the stratosphere, before descending to a final low, resolute tone. I felt my sophisticated interpretation would impress the formidable Starker.

János Starker was celebrated in the classical music world, his dazzling technique and ingenious musicality offered impeccably played beautiful music. But behind the scenes he was a narcissist, a misogynist, hard-edged. The music world overlooked his temper and snooty attitude. Ours was a culture that tolerated *prima donnas* with abrasive, reckless egos. It was a world where no one ever dared talk back.

'And dress nice,' my teacher said. 'You know what I mean.'

Yes, I knew. It meant either a skirt or low-cut dress. And, honestly? If placing the cello between my legs might offer some prurient appeal to the master, well, that was just creepy.

The day arrived, a Wednesday, and I pulled on black concert pants and a long-sleeved, high-collared white shirt. I entered the small studio with its steely fluorescent light, getting a look from my teacher when he saw my outfit.

Sitting a few feet away from my chair was the maestro himself, a gargoyle gazing at nothing. He nodded at me glumly, his face propped up with two fingers, and in his thick Hungarian accent he said, 'Vat ahh you playing vor me today?' I was just another young cellist he'd have to endure.

'She is playing a movement of the Ben Britten piece, maestro,' my teacher said.

I sat down, took a breath, and gripped my bow too tight, though I knew this would rob me of a relaxed sound. I got stuck on the first long low note as I tried to ground myself in the bass timbres. The soft, chromatic passages had to be lilting, tantalizing, had to pull the listener in.

Long held notes with watery vibratos were sonic mantras, begging the listener to ponder what would come next. By the second line, Starker crossed his legs and looked around; my bow arm wobbled and it felt like my hands were baseball mitts. The phrases expanded and the piece modulated to a different key, providing a sense of melancholy, the music getting louder and bolder, preparing for the climax. Starker shifted in his seat as I reached the loftier register, tackling a difficult passage of hurried notes I had worked on repeatedly.

And there I was, aloft, levitating in the sky on my high note, holding, savouring.

And then Starker lit a cigarette.

I froze, holding the high note (now a singular plea for my place in the music world) as a puff of smoke wafted over me. His insidious exhaust slowly dissipated, snuffing out something deep inside me.

My teacher hissed out, 'Go on!'

I eased off the high note, moved too fast through the final passages (sorry, Mr Britten!), robbing the finale of its sorrow and resignation. Who was this person playing? I was no longer a vibrant being passionately offering beautiful music, but a dismal, inert conduit for sound. I shortened the last note and Starker took another long drag.

I stood up quickly, sweaty, flushed, ready to flee, but Starker said, 'Vie don't you play voor me a C-sharp minor scale? Three octaves.'

It was the hardest scale in western music and, undoubtedly, I would fumble through, shaming and humiliating both myself and my teacher.

I looked at Starker, my heart pounding, and I heard myself say, 'Sorry. I don't play scales on Wednesdays.'

My teacher's mouth dropped open and I frantically lifted my cello, left the room, and headed aimlessly down the hall, wanting to dematerialise forever.

But my teacher, at my heels, screamed, 'Are you CRAZY? No one ever refuses the maestro!'

'Sorry,' I said, quickening my gait. 'I'm not going back there – that man isn't human.'

'This doesn't look good. At all!' he spun around and stomped away.

The János Starker moment with that fatal high note dramatically redefined my place in the school. Students I thought were friends now held me in disdain, landing me on the social black list. I was ignored, stared at, talked about behind my back. My cello remained in its case, untouched.

I was determined to put music behind me. I changed my major to journalism, where the emphasis was on thinking critically and students weren't being pushed to chase perfection but rather openly accept human frailty as an opportunity for learning. I avoided the music school at all costs and took different routes around campus so I didn't have to look at it.

But a request for me to submit my final transfer papers demanded a brief visit to the rotunda. I quietly walked inside, passing the recital hall where a stunning Beethoven quartet was being rehearsed. A voice inside me murmured, 'Remember me?'

Would I be able to leave the cello locked away forever?

Back in my room, I released the cello from solitary confinement, dusted it off, and plucked the out-of-tune strings, the dissonance souring the air. The least I could do was tune it.

The black ebony pegs wouldn't budge at first, so I clenched my teeth and managed to adjust the strings until the clarity of perfect intervals rang out. I placed the cello back in the corner and stared at it. My teeth were still clenched.

Had the smoke-infused high note indelibly marked the fissure between me and the music world? Had the challenge of performing under pressure made me lose my nerve once and for all?

I reached for the cello once more. Lifting it up, I felt its familiar weight and remembered school auditions, the thrill of acceptance, standing ovations at youth symphony performances. I remembered making it sing.

I plucked the strings loudly, the reverberations ringing out from the corner.

There's a Man in the Shadows

by Sheila Davie

'Hi Rach, just listen, will you? I need a favour. Can you get down to the cafe?'

The phone went dead. Blast, out of battery.

Busty Suzie landed his fry up on the table like a pilot training for an emergency landing, the eggs under just enough control to avert a major disaster.

'Hang on, Suzie, what's with you today?'

She went to the juke box, slipped in a token and sat down on a stool behind the counter. The slow soulful jazz was depressing this early in the morning.

Jonathan watched her as he ate. Was she on something? He mopped the greasy plate and ran a serviette around his mouth.

'OK, Suzie?'

She looked up, bleary-eyed, her face puffy and tired. The faint smile behind her eyes turned to fear when the track was switched off by the man he'd seen with Eloise. He looked like a nasty piece of work, and Suzie was scared.

Jonathan tried to distract her by ordering a mug of tea; he relocated to a table by the door. He wrote his phone number down on the menu and hoped she would notice when she brought his drink over.

The café door swung open. A familiar tap on the shoulder sent a shudder through his body stirring up all the old emotions.

'So, what's the big deal?' Rachel sat down, placing her phone on the table as if it were a recording machine. A reporter's habit. 'When the phone went dead I thought you were in trouble.'

'Nothing like that, Rach. Thanks for coming though. Phone ran out of juice. A tricky case, just good to have an ear to bend over it.'

'That's all?' Rachel asked. 'I had to make a good excuse to get away. James doesn't take prisoners.'

'How is the wonderful James Lander then? Did you know they'd asked me to do some freelance work?'

'You mentioned something about needing proof the other day, what was that supposed to mean? I can't give you inside information.'

'Nothing like that,' Jonathan replied. 'I wondered if you would proofread an article for me. You know what I'm like with grammar. I expect Mr Wonderful is word-perfect, is he?'

'Far from it, a bit scatty really, but he can sniff out a story anywhere and that's the main thing,' Rachel conceded. Then, 'Well, if that's all, I'm off.'

'Hang on, Rach, remember the Redbury Festival? Wouldn't it be fun, just for old time's sake? Take the bike and a tent?'

He could see that surprised her. She would remember the exhilaration of clinging on to him as they broke all the speed limits. Long nights in the tent, sometime days too. Tempting. He watched her face.

'Wait a minute,' he said.

The juke box swallowed his token, and his pride, as it changed beat, became animated, alive. Their song. The man with Suzie scowled and approached the juke box.

Rachel smiled, 'See you around, Jonathan.'

The track stopped. Jonathan paid his bill and left.

*

As luck would have it, *The Herald* asked Jonathan to cover the Redbury Festival, hotel accommodation thrown in. He needed the money. Since the Eloise case, he hadn't had a paid assignment, and he couldn't spend all his time following up the threatening note he'd been sent: 'Leave her alone or your toast.' He could mull that over in his spare time, he thought, although he already had an idea or two about who had sent it: even his grammar wasn't *that* bad.

A week later he checked into The Crown, on the outskirts of Redbury.

Jonathan noticed the receptionist giving him the once over: leathers, crash helmet. Not your normal hotel guest, but the Festival brought in all sorts. He took the stairs to room 26, he should have taken the lift.

As he drew on his inhaler, he noticed the room overlooked the car park: *The Herald* hadn't spared any expense, then. His meal allowance was just as meagre, so he ordered room service. Cod and chips: well, it was Friday night. It went down well with a couple of beers.

The bed was comfortable, a darn-sight better than the B&B he'd found himself staying in since he'd been made redundant. The sooner he got out of that place the better. He tried to fight off sleep as he watched the news, but soon gave in.

He woke up next morning with a stiff neck, children's Saturday morning TV blasting out, wondering where the hell he was, but not for long. He would be late for breakfast if he didn't get a move on.

He breezed into the restaurant. Shock horror, what was Rach doing here? Had she changed her mind? His heart skipped a beat, and then a few more when he saw Lander taking two fruit juices over to her table. He decided to give breakfast a miss and leave before they spotted him.

'Can I hitch a ride, it's my day off?' It was last night's receptionist.

He gave Rachel and Lander a backward look. 'Sure,' he said. 'See you in five minutes out front.'

She climbed on behind him, holding tight, then tighter as they shot off. He was caning it, a bit of a laugh, and he liked hearing her squeal. He accelerated like a bat out of hell wishing it was Rach pressing herself against him.

He dropped her off and went through security to the press stand. A bit of jostling going on for the free coffee and toast.

He was reminded of the note for a moment, *your toast*, then piled in to get his fill.

Like all the journalists there he hoped he could get a different angle on the festival, make a headline, give them something to think about at *The Herald*, make them wish they'd never got rid of him.

Nothing out of the ordinary yet. Some minor celebs warming up. Last-minute adjustments to unfinished stands. The perimeter fields were filling up with scruffy tents. No luxury here, either wanted or available, though he had spotted a blue and grey VW camper in its own little plot near where he'd parked his motorbike. In a few hours the site would be heaving, wall to wall sunshine was forecast. Nice work if you can get it.

An hour or two later, he caught a glimpse of his pillion

passenger in the crowd. She hadn't hung around when he dropped her off: places to go, people to see, she'd said. There was something vaguely familiar about her. She saw him and met his eye. Was she coming on to him, or was she on something? Then she was gone.

'Leave her alone or your toast.'

He looked around. Was someone following him?

It would have to wait. He had a four o'clock deadline for his article. He checked his watch, it was eleven-fifty. The festival was getting underway.

In prime position, the headline act was tuning up: The Jinx were on at midday to kick-start the programme. This group could make the big-time; local semi-professionals were always popular. They warmed up with some Suzie-style blues, then picked up the pace, drawing in a sizeable crowd. He was camera-ready for that perfect quirky shot.

'Sorry, mate,' someone said as they collided with the camera, sending the lens sideways as the shutter clicked.

He tried pushing through to get closer. Showing his press pass didn't help and he needed to be careful with the camera, it belonged to *The Herald*.

The Jinx turned up the amplifier. It was hot and he needed his puffer. Finding a way through, he went to the back of the stage where it was cooler. Closing his eyes, he inhaled. No time for relief, someone grabbed him from behind.

'Keep quiet.'

The man from the café.

One hand clutching the camera, the other forced up his back, Jonathan was pushed under the stage. He sensed what was coming. The man smashed his fist into Jonathan's face. Out like a light.

When he came to, he'd been bound and gagged. The Jinx

had long gone. Flashing lights stung his eyes, deafening music battered his eardrums. The stage boards above him were pulsing, creaking. He had no idea of the time, except that he must have missed his deadline. Only one shot on the camera and that was off-piste. Talking of which, he needed a pee.

A brief pause in the rhythm as the next band was introduced. His attempt at a muffled shout inaudible.

There's a man in the shadows
With a gun in his eye
There's evil in the air
But I gotta get out

He tried to be rational. Two things were certain: he hadn't met his deadline, and he was out of his depth.

Unable to hold the pee in any longer, he rolled over to be more comfortable. Something soft brushed against him. Shallow breathing, delicate perfume.

He thought of the note. 'Leave her alone or your toast.'

There's a man in the shadows.

About the Authors

Jan Brown is still refining her writing skills and enjoying writing flash fiction, without dreaming of The Big Novel.

Sheila Davie was brought up on a farm in rural Kent; she then lived in Cheshire for 30 years bringing up a family and later working as an HR Director.

Mike Evis lives just outside Oxford, England. has a long-standing interest in writing, plus an inability to pass any bookshop without entering and buying something.

Margaret Gallop: I have always enjoyed writing, teaching creative writing and poetry with children and adults, and helping people put their stories into words.

David Hamilton: if I think I'm sending dynamite, the judges survive. If I enter just to support competitions, I sometimes do better.

Colin Heaney: twenty-one-year-old university student and avid read. Coffee addict, music lover, pizza killer.

Camilla Johansson is a Swedish journalist writing fiction in English. She lives in the Swedish countryside with her son.

Alice Lam writes fiction with a passion for the psyche's shadow side. Her website is found at alicelambooks.com.

Alice Little enjoys writing of all kinds and has had a number of short stories published in print and online. This is the second anthology she has edited for Didcot Writers. Find out more at alicelittle.co.uk/fiction.

Abby Luby, a journalist, has written for *The New York Daily News*, *SolveClimateNews*, *The Villager*, and *The Real Deal*, among others.

Matthew C. McLean is a writer living in North Carolina.

Amy Mutha believes that everyone has a story worth telling.

Zoe Reed: I am a PhD student in Epidemiology but have always loved writing, although this is my first competition.

Mary Walter: music has always played a big part in my life and as I enjoy writing I have blended the two.

14195599R00058

Printed in Great Britain
by Amazon